TINTERN ABBEY
ODE TO DUTY 40114
ODE ON INTIMATIONS OF IMMORTALITY
THE HAPPY WARRIOR
RESOLUTION AND INDEPENDENCE

AND

ON THE POWER OF SOUND

BY

WILLIAM WORDSWORTH

With Life and Notes

By ALEX. M. TROTTER, M.A.

W & R. CHAMBERS, LIMITED
LONDON AND EDINBURGH
1892

CONTENTS.

LIFE OF WORDSWORTH.

WILLIAM WORDSWORTH, son of the law agent on the estates of the first Earl of Lonsdale, was born at Cockermouth, in Cumberland, on the 7th April 1770. He was first sent to school at Penrith; but, after the death of his mother in 1778, he was transferred to the public school at Hawkshead, in Lancashire, where he completed his earlier education. His father's death in 1783 left the family in straitened circumstances, Lord Lonsdale having refused to pay a considerable sum of money due to them. In 1787 he was entered at St John's College, Cambridge, where in 1791 he passed his examination for the degree of B.A. During the previous year he made, with a fellow-student, a pedestrian tour through France, then in the first wild hopes of the Revolution. With the aspirations of the Republican party he at first ardently sympathised, but the subsequent excesses of the revolutionists completely alienated him from the cause.

In 1793, Wordsworth came before the public as an author, in two poems entitled *The Evening Walk* and *Descriptive Sketches*. In 1795, an intimate friend, named Calvert, died and bequeathed to the poet £900—a sum which enabled him, with his attached sister Dorothy, to settle in comfort at Racedown Lodge, in Dorsetshire. Two years afterwards he removed to Alfoxden, in Somersetshire, where he enjoyed the friendship of Coleridge. To this period belong the *Lyrical Ballads*, a joint adventure of the two poets, which did not prove remunerative. After a short tour in Germany, along with his sister and Coleridge, Wordsworth returned to his native Cumberland, which he never again permanently left. He settled first at Grasmere; in 1808, he removed to Allan Bank, in the vicinity; and in 1813, he transferred his household to Rydal Mount, where he spent the remainder of his life. In 1802, his claim against the Lonsdale estates was admitted, and he received £8000; and in the same year he married his cousin, Mary Hutchinson, with whom he had been intimate from childhood. In 1813 he was appointed Distributor of Stamps for the county of Westmorland, with a salary of £500 a year.

He received a pension from the Crown in 1842; and in the following year, on the death of his friend Southey, he was appointed Poet-Laureate. He died full of years and honour on the 23d April 1850. His chief poems are—*Lyrical Ballads* (1798), *Tintern Abbey* (1798), *The Excursion* (1814), *The White Doe of Rylstone* (1815), *Sonnets* (1820), and *The Prelude* (published in 1850).

The principal object which Wordsworth proposed to himself in his early poems, was to choose incidents and situations from ordinary life, and to relate or describe them in the language commonly used by men; at the same time investing them with a certain colouring of the imagination, whereby ordinary things should be presented to the mind in an unusual way; and it was his aim further, and above all, to make these incidents and situations interesting, by tracing in them the primary laws of our nature. His *Excursion*, which is only part of a larger and unpublished work, entitled *The Recluse*, is one of the noblest philosophical poems in our language; containing views at once comprehensive and simple, of man, nature, and society, and combining the finest sensibilities with the richest fancy. Nor can any poems more deeply touching be found than *The Fountain*, *Ruth*, *We are Seven*, *The Complaint of the Indian*, and others of his minor pieces. He indeed possessed, in an eminent degree, the grand qualification of a poet, as described by himself: 'a promptness greater than what is possessed by ordinary men, to think and feel without immediate excitement, and a greater power of expressing such thoughts and feeling as are produced in him in that manner.'

WORDSWORTH.

LINES

COMPOSED A FEW MILES ABOVE TINTERN ABBEY, ON REVISITING
THE BANKS OF THE WYE DURING A TOUR.

JULY 13, 1798.

[Tintern Abbey is a famous ecclesiastical ruin on the right bank of the Wye,
in Monmouthshire, a few miles south-east of the town of Monmouth. It owes
most of its celebrity to this poem.

The Wye takes its origin from two copious springs which issue from the side
of Plinlimmon, and joins the Severn two and a half miles below Chepstow.
The part of the river chiefly visited for its grand and picturesque scenery is
that between Monmouth and Chepstow.]

> FIVE years have passed ; five summers, with the length
> Of five long winters ! and again I hear
> These waters, rolling from their mountain-springs
> With a soft inland murmur.—Once again
> Do I behold these steep and lofty cliffs,　　　　　　　　　5
> That on a wild secluded scene impress
> Thoughts of more deep seclusion ; and connect
> The landscape with the quiet of the sky.

ABBREVIATIONS.—A.S. = Anglo-Saxon ; Cf. = compare (Latin, *confer*) ;
Fr. = French ; Gr. = Greek ; Icel. = Icelandic ; Lat. = Latin ; lit. = literally ;
M.E. = Middle English (from 13th to 15th century).

LINE

4. **Soft inland murmur**, in contrast
with the rush and roar of the river, as
it dashes over its rocky channel near
its junction with the Severn.

5. **Cliffs**, steep rocks. A.S. *clif*, a
rock ; lit. 'a climbing-place,' from
clifian, to adhere, to cleave to.

6–8. The scene is *wild*—it owes
nothing to art : it is *secluded*, being far
from the haunts of man ; and the bold

cliffs towering, as it were, to the silent
heavens above, impart to it a character
which deepens still more the visitor's
sense of isolation.

8. **Landscape**, the aspect of the
country. The word was first used by
the Dutch painters. Dutch, *landschap*,
the *form* or fashion of the *land*. The
suffix *-schap* corresponds to the A.S.
-scipe, and the Modern English *-ship* in
'friendship.'

The day is come when I again repose
Here, under this dark sycamore, and view   10
These plots of cottage-ground, these orchard-tufts,
Which at this season, with their unripe fruits,
Are clad in one green hue, and lose themselves
'Mid groves and copses.   Once again I see
These hedgerows, hardly hedgerows, little lines   15
Of sportive wood run wild : these pastoral farms,
Green to the very door ; and wreaths of smoke
Sent up, in silence, from among the trees !
With some uncertain notice, as might seem
Of vagrant dwellers in the houseless woods,   20
Or of some Hermit's cave, where by his fire
The Hermit sits alone.
                              These beauteous forms,
Through a long absence, have not been to me
As is a landscape to a blind man's eye :
But oft, in lonely rooms, and 'mid the din   25
Of towns and cities, I have owed to them,
In hours of weariness, sensations sweet,
Felt in the blood, and felt along the heart ;

10. Dark, with thick foliage.——
Sycamore, Gr. *sykomŏros*, the 'fig-
mulberry'—*sykon*, a fig, and *moron*, a
mulberry.   The sycamore of Britain is
a kind of maple, called in Scotland the
plane-tree.

11. Orchard, lit. 'herb-garden.'
A.S. *wyrt*, a plant; *geard*, an in-
closure.——Tuft, knot, cluster. Fr.
touffe, a tuft : the final *t* is excrescent.
——Orchard-tufts, clusters of fruit
trees.

13. These have all the same green
hue, and cannot be distinguished in
colour from the groves and copses in
their vicinity.

14. Grove, a collection of trees.
A.S. *gráf*, a grove or glade, from
grafan, to cut.——Copse, a plantation ;
lit. underwood frequently cut. O. Fr.
copeiz; Fr. *couper*, to cut.

15. Hedgerows [which are] hardly
hedgerows [but rather] lines. . . .
Hedge, a fence. A.S. *haga*, an in-

closure.   Cog. *haw* (the berry), *haw
haw* (a sunk fence), *hawthorn*.

16. Sportive, straggling, untrimmed.
Cf. 'Beside yon straggling fence that
skirts the way.'—*Deserted Village*.

19. The curling smoke rising silently
among the trees, vaguely indicates the
presence of man.

20. Vagrant dwellers, wanderers,
as gipsies, who have selected this spot
as a temporary resting-place.

21. Hermit, a solitary. M.E.
heremite, through the Fr. and Lat.
from Gr. *erêmos*, deserted, desolate.

23. During the five years of his
absence from the 'silvan Wye,' the
poet has ever cherished the memory of
its beautiful scenery.

24. A landscape is a mere blank to
a blind man's eye.

25-30. During seasons of weariness
and depression, both in the silent
retirement of his home, and amid the
noise and bustle of the streets, the

And passing even into my purer mind,
With tranquil restoration :—feelings too   30
Of unremembered pleasure : such, perhaps,
As have no slight or trivial influence
On that best portion of a good man's life,
His little, nameless, unremembered, acts
Of kindness and of love.   Nor less, I trust,   35
To them I may have owed another gift,
Of aspect more sublime ; that blessed mood,
In which the burthen of the mystery,
In which the heavy and the weary weight
Of all this unintelligible world,   40
Is lightened :—that serene and blessed mood,
In which the affections gently lead us on,—
Until, the breath of this corporeal frame
And even the motion of our human blood
Almost suspended, we are laid asleep   45

recollection of these 'beauteous forms' has cheered and refreshed him in body ('blood'), in soul ('heart'), and in spirit ('purer mind').

30. With tranquil restoration, with soothing and reviving power. Cf. 'healing thoughts,' line 144.

Compare what Wordsworth says of his remembrance of the 'dancing daffodils:'

'Oft, when on my couch I lie
  In vacant or in pensive mood,
They flash upon that inward eye
  Which is the bliss of solitude ;
And then my heart with pleasure fills,
  And dances with the daffodils.'
                        Daffodils.

——Before 'feelings too' supply 'I have owed to them.'

31–35. A loving communion with Nature, especially in her gentler and more winning aspects, tends to chasten and humanise the soul : it moderates the passions, widens the sympathies, and fosters a spirit of tenderness and charity which recognises the universal brotherhood of man. To his former intercourse with these 'beauteous

forms,' the poet attributes an effect of this kind—a benign, though perhaps unconscious, influence over many acts of daily life.

32. Slight, unimportant; lit. smooth, flat. Old Dutch, *slicht*, even, plain. ——**Trivial,** common. Lat. *trivialis* (*tres*, three, *via*, a way), belonging to three cross-roads, that which may be picked up anywhere, common.

34. Acts, in apposition to 'that best portion.'

37. Of aspect more sublime, of a higher kind.——**Mood,** state of mind. A.S. *môd,* mind, feeling. 'Mood,' meaning 'manner,' is from Lat. *môdus*, a measure, a way.

38. Mystery, hidden meaning. Gr. *mysterion*, a secret rite : *mueo*, to initiate. In this high poetic mood, the veil is withdrawn from the 'unintelligible world,' and the inner nature and meaning of things are revealed.

42. Affections, the higher emotional nature.

43. Corporeal frame, the body.

43–45. The breath. . . . suspended, an absolute construction. 'Freed from the bonds of sense, the soul rises to communion with the spirit that works

In body, and become a living soul :
While with an eye made quiet by the power
Of harmony, and the deep power of joy,
We see into the life of things.
                                        If this
Be but a vain belief, yet, oh! how oft—   50
In darkness and amid the many shapes
Of joyless daylight ; when the fretful stir
Unprofitable, and the fever of the world,
Have hung upon the beatings of my heart—
How oft, in spirit, have I turned to thee,   55
O silvan Wye! thou wanderer through the woods,
How often has my spirit turned to thee !
And now, with gleams of half-extinguished thought,
With many recognitions dim and faint,
And somewhat of a sad perplexity,   60
The picture of the mind revives again :
While here I stand, not only with the sense
Of present pleasure, but with pleasing thoughts
That in this moment there is life and food
For future years.   And so I dare to hope,   65
Though changed, no doubt, from what I was when first

harmoniously in nature, and with clear vision and intense joy beholds the inner life of things.'

50-57. The poet may be wrong, though he believes himself to be right, in attributing this lofty mood to the influence of these 'beauteous forms' treasured within his memory; he is certain, at anyrate, of this, that amid the dreariness of life and the profitless excitement of worldly pursuits, his spirit has been often cheered and tranquillised by recalling the quiet beauty of the scene before him.

52. Joyless daylight, day that brings no joy.——Fretful stir, restless and wearing agitation. Fret, lit. gnaw: from A.S. *fretan*, contracted from *for-etan*, to eat away; hence, to vex.

54. Have hung upon, so as to retard; 'have oppressed my heart.'

58-65. Standing once more in presence of these beauteous forms, the poet recalls the ideal picture of them which he has cherished for so many years. He finds that many of the thoughts and feelings awakened by them on his former visit have almost faded from recollection, and now come back to him with dim, blurred outline and painful uncertainty. Still, as before, his sensations are of a pleasurable character, and from the memory of these too, in future years, he ventures to hope that he will reap much spiritual benefit.

60. Of a sad perplexity, sadly perplexing, painfully confused: an adjective phrase, co-ordinate with 'dim and faint,' qualifying 'recognitions,' and modified by 'somewhat.'

65. So = 'that in this moment there is life,' &c.

66. Though [I am] changed. . . . His mental and emotional nature had

I came among these hills : when like a roe
I bounded o'er the mountains, by the sides
Of the deep rivers, and the lonely streams,
Wherever nature led : more like a man　　　　70
Flying from something that he dreads, than one
Who sought the thing he loved.　For nature then
(The coarser pleasures of my boyish days,
And their glad animal movements all gone by)
To me was all in all.—I cannot paint　　　　75
What then I was.　The sounding cataract
Haunted me like a passion : the tall rock,
The mountain, and the deep and gloomy wood,
Their colours and their forms, were then to me
An appetite ; a feeling and a love,　　　　80
That had no need of a remoter charm,
By thought supplied, nor any interest
Unborrowed from the eye.—That time is past,
And all its aching joys are now no more,
And all its dizzy raptures.　Not for this　　　　85
Faint I, nor mourn nor murmur ; other gifts
Have followed ; for such loss, I would believe,
Abundant recompense.　For I have learned

necessarily changed with the lapse of years, and therefore he could not contemplate the beauties around him with the same feelings as before (cf. line 88).

73. Coarser, less refined.　He refers to his boyish delight in exercise and adventure.

74. Glad animal movements, boyish vivacity of temperament ; the happiness arising from mere animal existence.

75. All in all, everything desired. ——Paint, describe.

76. Cataract, waterfall ; lit. the rushing down of broken water.　Gr. *kata*, down, *rhēgnumi*, I break.

77. Haunted me like a passion, 'took abiding possession of my soul.' 'Haunt,' M.E. *haunten*; O. Fr. *hanter*, to frequent.

80. Appetite, a strong desire or craving.——A feeling and a love, in apposition to 'appetite.' 'Appetite'

is here used by metonymy for 'object of desire ;' the grand forms and glowing colours of nature satisfy his eyes as food satisfies hunger.

81–83. The loveliness of nature—the mere charm of her visible presence—was enough to fill him with intense delight.

83–102. The poet does not regret that this season of imperfect intercourse with nature, with all its intensity of joy, has passed away ; for it has been to him but the prelude and preparation for a higher and more intimate communion.　Cf. *Ode on Immortality*, lines 177–186.

84. Aching joys, painful intensity of joy.　Joy may be so intense as to cause pain.　This is an example of the figure *oxymoron*, which consists in joining words that are contradictory, or in qualifying a noun with an adjective that really quenches its meaning, as ' idly busy,' ' cruel kindness.'

B

To look on nature, not as in the hour
Of thoughtless youth; but hearing oftentimes   90
The still, sad music of humanity,
Nor harsh nor grating, though of ample power
To chasten and subdue. And I have felt
A presence that disturbs me with the joy
Of elevated thoughts; a sense sublime   95
Of something far more deeply interfused,
Whose dwelling is the light of setting suns,
And the round ocean and the living air,
And the blue sky, and in the mind of man :
A motion and a spirit, that impels   100
All thinking things, all objects of all thought,
And rolls through all things. Therefore am I still
A lover of the meadows and the woods
And mountains ; and of all that we behold
From this green earth ; of all the mighty world   105
Of eye and ear—both what they half-create,
And what perceive ; well pleased to recognise

89. **Not as** [I looked on nature] in the hour . . .

90-93. One feature of this loftier mood to which he had attained, is that a strain of human interest constantly mingles with the delight derived from impersonal things. His love for nature led him to love and reverence for man. Cf. *Ode on Immortality*, lines 183, 184.

92. [Which is] **nor harsh nor grating, though** [it is] **of ample power.**

93. **Chasten,** to free from error or fault, to purify. Lat. *castus*, pure. ——**Subdue,** to overcome, to melt to tenderness. Lat. *sub*, under, *ducere*, to bring.

93-102. In this serene mood, the poet, filled with the joy of lofty thoughts, becomes conscious of a presence in nature, a mighty spirit which pervades the universe and manifests itself everywhere in beauty and in power.

95. **Sense sublime,** lofty feeling or consciousness.

100. **A motion and a spirit.** In apposition to 'something' in line 96. In a poem on the *Influence of Natural Objects*, Wordsworth addresses the Wisdom and Spirit of the Universe, ' that gives to forms and images a breath and everlasting motion.'—— **Impels,** moves, animates.

101. 'All things animate and inanimate.'

102. **Still,** that is, ' though changed from what I was' (line 66).

105. **The mighty world of eye and ear,** every sight and every sound ; the vast world of things visible and audible.

106. **They,** that is, the eye and ear. ——**Half-create.** Sights and sounds do not always present themselves to the eye and ear as they really exist in nature, but invested, as it were, with some special quality that is due to the condition of the senses at the moment. In this sense, the eye and ear may be said to ' half-create' these objects of sensation.

107. [I am] **well pleased** . . .

In nature and the language of the sense,
The anchor of my purest thoughts, the nurse,
The guide, the guardian of my heart, and soul   110
Of all my moral being.
                   Nor perchance,
If I were not thus taught, should I the more.
Suffer my genial spirits to decay :
For thou art with me here upon the banks
Of this fair river ; thou my dearest Friend,   115
My dear, dear Friend ; and in thy voice I catch
The language of my former heart, and read
My former pleasures in the shooting lights
Of thy wild eyes.   Oh ! yet a little while
May I behold in thee what I was once,   120
My dear, dear Sister ! and this prayer I make
Knowing that Nature never did betray
The heart that loved her ; 'tis her privilege,
Through all the years of this our life, to lead
From joy to joy : for she can so inform   125
The mind that is within us, so impress
With quietness and beauty, and so feed
With lofty thoughts, that neither evil tongues,

---

108. The language of the sense, the knowledge of external objects conveyed by the senses. 'I am rejoiced to feel that there is in nature· and the knowledge of nature an influence to keep me true to my noblest conceptions, to foster, direct, and guard my best affections, and to preserve within me a calm and quiet conscience.'

112. 'Even if I had not learned to contemplate nature in a sympathetic, meditative, and devout spirit.'—— **Thus,** refers to lines 88-102.

113. Genial spirits, natural cheerfulness of disposition. Lat. *genialis,* pleasant ; *genius,* the good attendant spirit of one's life.

114. Thou, his only sister, Dorothy, to whom he was tenderly attached, and who, to the day of her death, was his constant and congenial companion. She, too, was an ardent lover of nature ; and as she gazes with him now on the scenery of the 'silvan Wye,' he discerns in her gleaming eyes the glow of those 'dizzy raptures' by which, in earlier years, his own soul had been moved in presence of these beauteous forms ; and he anticipates for her what he had himself received—that lofty mood which unites profound emotion with intense repose.

122. 'Nature never deserts or proves faithless to her worshipper.'

123. Privilege, a right she enjoys and exercises. Lat. *privilegium,* a *law* regarding a *single* person— *privus,* single ; *lex,* a law.

125. From 'aching joy' (line 84) to the chastened 'joy of elevated thoughts' (line 94).——**Inform,** give form to, mould.

126, 127. Impress, stamp ; **feed,** nourish and strengthen. These verbs are transitive, their object being 'mind.'

Rash judgments, nor the sneers of selfish men,
Nor greetings where no kindness is, nor all   130
The dreary intercourse of daily life,
Shall e'er prevail against us, or disturb
Our cheerful faith that all which we behold
Is full of blessings.   Therefore let the moon
Shine on thee in thy solitary walk ;   135
And let the misty mountain-winds be free
To blow against thee : and, in after-years,
When these wild ecstasies shall be matured
Into a sober pleasure ; when thy mind
Shall be a mansion for all lovely forms,   140
Thy memory be as a dwelling-place
For all sweet sounds and harmonies ; oh ! then,
If solitude, or fear, or pain, or grief,
Should be thy portion, with what healing thoughts
Of tender joy wilt thou remember me,   145
And these my exhortations !   Nor, perchance—
If I should be where I no more can hear
Thy voice, nor catch from thy wild eyes these gleams
Of past existence—wilt thou then forget
That on the banks of this delightful stream   150
We stood together ; and that I, so long
A worshipper of Nature, hither came

129. **Rash**, hasty and ill-founded.

130. **Greetings**, salutations, professions of kindly interest. A.S. *grétan*, visit, address.——**Where** = in which.

182. ' Or deprive us of the cheering conviction that ' . . .

184. **Therefore**, that is, ' since this is the result of communion with nature.'

138. **Wild ecstasies**, ' dizzy raptures ' (line 85), intense joy. Gr. *ek*, out, *stasis*, a standing. Cf. ' transport,' that which *carries* us, ' rapture ' or ' ravishment,' that which *snatches* us out of and above ourselves.

139. **Sober**, quiet, subdued ; opposed to ' *wild* ecstasies.' Lat. *se*, apart, not ; *ebrius*, drunk.

140. **Mansion**, abiding-place. Lat. *manēre*, to remain.

148. ' How mournfully, ere life ended, were those wild eyes darkened !' Miss Wordsworth's passion for nature led her into mountain rambles, which were beyond her strength. ' In 1832, she had a serious illness, which left her with her intellect painfully impaired, and her bright nature permanently overclouded.'—Myers, *Wordsworth.*

144. **Healing**, consolatory. Her memory thus richly stored, and her heart and mind thus moulded by nature, she would have within her an unfailing source of consolation in hours of solitude and distress.

149. **Of past existence**, that is, which remind me of what I once thought and felt. Cf. lines 115-117.

151. **That I** [who had been] **so** long . . .

Unwearied in that service : rather say
With warmer love—oh ! with far deeper zeal
Of holier love.   Nor wilt thou then forget,   155
That after many wanderings, many years
Of absence, these steep woods and lofty cliffs,
And this green pastoral landscape, were to me
More dear, both for themselves and for thy sake !

ODE TO DUTY.

Jam non consilio bonus, sed more eò perductus, ut non tantum rectè facere
possim, sed nisi rectè facere non possim.'

[This Ode, written in 1805, has for its model Gray's *Ode to Adversity*, which
begins :

'Daughter of Jove, relentless power,
Thou tamer of the human breast.'

The Latin motto means, ' No longer good by resolve, but so educated by habit,
that not only am I able to act rightly, but I am unable to act otherwise than
rightly.]

STERN Daughter of the Voice of God !
O Duty ! if that name thou love
Who art a light to guide, a rod
. To check the erring, and reprove ;
╰Thou, who art victory and law   5
When empty terrors overawe ;

153. Rather say [that I came] with . . .

159. For thy sake, that is, because he knew that they would be to her, as they had been to him, a source of blessing.

1. Stern, inexorable, relentless.—— **Voice of God**, expression of the Divine will.   Duty, the impersonation to us of the immutable will of God, instructs the ignorant ('a light to guide'), and restrains and corrects the erring ('a rod ').

2-4. If that name . . . reprove. A complex conditional clause parenthetical.——**That name**, namely, 'Duty.'——Duty (Lat. *debère*, to owe);

lit. ' what we ought to do'—a code of right actions.   Here it means the divine power which prescribes right actions.   Within us this power is represented by conscience, which has been called ' God's vicegerent in the soul.'

5-8. Thou is subject of ' dost set.' He who is guided by duty has a courage, protection, and repose of soul unknown to those who act as the humour or interest of the moment dictates.   The powers of evil threaten him in vain ; temptations have no power to allure him from the right path ; and he feels within himself ' a peace above all earthly dignities—a still and quiet conscience.'

From vain temptations dost set free ;
And calm'st the weary strife of frail humanity !

There are who ask not if thine eye
Be on them ; who, in love and truth,   10
Where no misgiving is, rely
Upon the genial sense of youth :
Glad hearts ! without reproach or blot ;
Who do thy work, and know it not :
Oh ! if through confidence misplaced   15
They fail, thy saving arms, dread Power ! around them cast.

Serene will be our days and bright,
And happy will our nature be,
When love is an unerring light,
And joy its own security.   20
And they a blissful course may hold,
Even now, who, not unwisely bold,
Live in the spirit of this creed ;
Yet seek thy firm support, according to their need.

---

8. Frail, morally weak. Lat. *fragilis*, easily broken, through Fr. *frêle*.

9. There are [some] **who . . .** Some are so amiable and unselfish by nature, that they *instinctively* do what is right.

10-12. 'Who, naturally loving and sincere, and therefore not troubled by doubts as to their conduct, obey those spontaneous and generous impulses ("genial sense") which mark the season of youth.'

11. Where = in which. —— **Rely upon,** trust to, as guides of conduct. Lat. *re-*, back ; A.S. *licgan*, to lie.

12. Genial sense—innate perception or intuition of what is right. Lat. *genius*, 'inborn faculty.'

13. Arrange : 'Who, glad hearts, without reproach or blot, do thy work.' —— **Reproach,** self-reproach; **without blot,** stainless, sincere.

14. And know it not, without knowing it, unconsciously.——It, that is, 'that they are doing it.'

15. If . . . 'If, at any time, it should prove that they have been wrong in trusting to their natural instincts.'

19, 20. 'So long as the love to which we trust is a faithful guide, and the pleasure which accompanies our actions is not mingled with misgivings or regret.' Cf. 'unreproved pleasures' in Milton's *L'Allegro*, line 40.

19. Unerring, and **own** in the next line, are emphatic.

20. Security, lit. 'freedom from care or anxiety.'

21. 'They may go on prosperously, without swerving from the right course.' A ship 'holds its course' when it sails exactly in the direction intended by the steersman.

22. Even now, even in this life.—— **Who** = 'if they.'——**Not unwisely bold,** without placing too much reliance on their own emotional instincts.

23. Creed, conviction ; lit. 'what is believed.' The creed (lines 19, 20) is, that joy and love are competent and trustworthy guides of conduct. The

I, loving freedom, and untried ;   25
No sport of every random gust,
Yet being to myself a guide,
Too blindly have reposed my trust :
And oft, when in my heart was heard
Thy timely mandate, I deferred   30
The task, in smoother walks to stray ;
But thee I now would serve more strictly, if I may.

Through no disturbance of my soul,
Or strong compunction in me wrought,
I supplicate for thy control ;   35
But in the quietness of thought :
Me this unchartered freedom tires ;
I feel the weight of chance-desires :
My hopes no more must change their name,
I long for a repose that ever is the same.   40

Stern Lawgiver ! yet thou dost wear
The Godhead's most benignant grace ;

meaning is: 'Who, though they act generally in accordance with this conviction, are yet, on occasions of doubt or misgiving ("according to their need") ready to appeal to the divine standard of duty.'

25. Loving freedom . . . guide— enlargement of subject 'I.'——**Untried,** untested, unexperienced.

26. 'Though not liable to be swayed by every "chance-desire"' (line 38), that is, though possessed of a certain amount of rational self-control.—— **Random,** chance, hazard. O. Fr. *randon,* the force and swiftness of a great stream.——**Gust,** sudden blast. Icel. *gusa,* to gush.

27. Blindly, implicitly, without reasoning or consideration.——**My trust,** confidence in my natural impulses.

30, 31. 'I put off the unpleasant task assigned me by duty, and preferred the easier and more agreeable course suggested by my own inclination.'——**Stray,** wander. O. Fr.

estraier, to rove about the *streets ;* Lat. *strata,* a street.

32. If I may, if it be still possible for me.

33–36. 'Not from any violent agitation of soul, not from any feeling of uneasiness caused by a reproving conscience, but after calm and serious deliberation, I ask thy guidance.'

36. Thought, deliberate consideration, as opposed to passion ('disturbance') and regret ('compunction').

37. 'I am weary of the unauthorised freedom in which I have hitherto lived.'——**Unchartered ;** Lat. *charta,* a paper. A *charter* is a document conferring a right or privilege. Duty, and not our natural instincts, is the *authoritative* guide of conduct.

38. In another poem Wordsworth speaks of souls 'who have felt the weight of too much liberty.'

41–48. Moral law and physical law are manifestations of the same divine power : both are 'daughters of the

Nor know we anything so fair
As is the smile upon thy face :
Flowers laugh before thee on their beds   45
And fragrance in thy footing treads ;
Thou dost preserve the stars from wrong ;
And the most ancient heavens, through Thee, are fresh and ·
        strong.

To humbler functions, awful Power !
I call thee : I myself commend   50
Unto thy guidance from this hour ;
Oh, let my weakness have an end !
Give unto me, made lowly wise,
The spirit of self-sacrifice ;
The confidence of reason give ;   55
And in the light of truth thy Bondman let me live !

voice of God.' And they are equally stern : they demand perfect obedience, and will not be satisfied with anything short of that. But this sternness is but benevolence—the loving regard of the Creator for the work of His hand ; for obedience is peace and order ; disobedience, anarchy and confusion. No human joy can be compared to that which springs from the smile of duty—the testimony of a good conscience ; and it is because the laws of nature are obeyed, that the universe presents a scene of harmony and beauty—the fragrant flowers blossoming in their season, the planets revolving in their appointed orbits, the starry heavens, as 'fresh and strong' as when they were called into being.

41. [Thou art a] stern lawgiver, yet . . .

47. Wrong, wandering, error. A.S. *wringan*, to twist or turn. Cf.

'right,' from Lat. *rectus*, drawn in a straight line.

48. Most ancient, very ancient. The superlative is used in an *absolute* sense.

49. Humbler, that is, than that of sustaining the universe. The humbler task is 'to guide me.'

53. Made lowly wise, made humble and wise.

54. The spirit of self-sacrifice, a disposition to disregard one's own desires and inclinations, and submit unreservedly to the guidance of duty.

55. Confidence of reason, as opposed to 'confidence misplaced' in his own nature.

56. 'We are born subjects,' says Seneca, 'and to obey is perfect liberty.' The *slaves* of duty are the only true *freemen*.——In the light of truth, guided by the truth.——Bondman is in apposition to 'me.'

ODE.

INTIMATIONS OF IMMORTALITY

FROM RECOLLECTIONS OF EARLY CHILDHOOD.

> 'The Child is father of the Man;
> And I could wish my days to be
> Bound each to each by natural piety.'

[This poem was written by Wordsworth during his residence at Grasmere, the first four stanzas in 1803, and the remainder at least two years afterwards. Its key-note is suggested in the motto prefixed, which is taken from one of Wordsworth's own earlier and shorter poems.

The ode is a poetical rendering of the famous doctrine of the pre-existence of the soul, a belief common in the East, but in European thought associated especially with the name of Plato. The doctrine implies that human souls were in existence, possibly in a higher and better state, before they became united with the bodies to which they are in this life attached. Hence the child has a sense of nearness to the spiritual world, which recedes and grows dim as he advances to manhood; and hence, too, much of the best knowledge that a man attains to is but 'recollection' of truths known by the soul in its pre-existent state, or, in the Christian form of the doctrine, of the spiritual light of that heavenly home which at birth we forsook, and to which at death we shall return.]

I.

THERE was a time when meadow, grove, and stream,
The earth, and every common sight,
          To me did seem
     Apparelled in celestial light,
The glory and the freshness of a dream.   5
It is not now as it hath been of yore;—
     Turn wheresoe'er I may,
          By night or day,
The things which I have seen I now can see no more.

I. To the poet, in his childhood, all nature seemed invested with dream-like vividness and splendour; now, in his manhood, this glory has faded.

1. 'Meadow,' 'grove,' 'stream,' 'earth,' 'sight' form a collective subject to 'did seem.'

4. **Apparelled**, arrayed, invested. O. Fr. *a*, to; *parailler*, to put *like* things with *like*; Lat. *ad*, to; *par*, equal, like.

5. **Glory** (= splendour), **freshness**, (= vividness, liveliness)—in apposition to 'light.'

6. **Of yore**, formerly. A.S. *geāra*, 'of years'—gen. pl. of *gear*, a year.

7. [Though I] **turn wheresoe'er I** may [turn].

C

II.

The Rainbow comes and goes,   10
And lovely is the Rose;
The Moon doth with delight
Look round her when the heavens are bare;
Waters on a starry night
Are beautiful and fair;   15
The sunshine is a glorious birth:
But yet I know, where'er I go,
That there hath passed away a glory from the earth.

III.

Now, while the birds thus sing a joyous song,
And while the young lambs bound   20
As to the tabor's sound,
To me alone there came a thought of grief:
A timely utterance gave that thought relief,
And I again am strong:
The cataracts blow their trumpets from the steep: 25
No more shall grief of mine the season wrong;
I hear the Echoes through the mountains throng,
The Winds come to me from the fields of sleep,
And all the earth is gay;
Land and sea   30
Give themselves up to jollity,

II. The objects of nature, though they have lost this charm, are still beautiful.

10. Comes and goes, appears and disappears.

13. The heavens are bare, the sky is clear and cloudless.

16. Birth, something born, thing.

18. Connect 'from the earth' with 'hath passed.'

III. While all around him is joy, this feeling of loss—of 'something gone'—brings a thought of sadness to the poet; but the expression of his experience has given him relief, and he resolves to banish gloom.

20. Bound, gambol, frisk. Fr. *bondir*, to leap.

21. As [if they bounded] to ....
——Tabor, a small drum. Fr. *tambour*, probably of imitative origin and allied to 'tap.'

25. Cataract, cascade, waterfall. Gr. *kata*, down, *rhêgnumi*, I break. He refers to the roar of the waters dashing over the precipices ('steep').

26. Melancholy thoughts are out of harmony with the general joy of Spring.

28. Fields of sleep, sleeping fields; it is early morning, and the fields have not yet awakened, as it were, from their slumber.

31. Jollity, mirth, festivity. Fr. *joli*, gay, fine. Icel. *jól*, a great feast in the heathen time; cognate with A.S. *geóla*, yule.

And with the heart of May
  Doth every Beast keep holiday ;—
   Thou Child of Joy,
Shout round me, let me hear thy shouts, thou happy Shepherd-
    boy !   35

IV.

Ye blessed Creatures, I have heard the call
  Ye to each other make ; I see
The heavens laugh with you in your jubilee ;
  My heart is at your festival,
   My head hath its coronal,   40
The fullness of your bliss, I feel—I feel it all.
   Oh evil day ! if I were sullen
   While Earth herself is adorning,
    This sweet May-morning,
   And the Children are culling   45
    On every side,
  In a thousand valleys far and wide,
  Fresh flowers ; while the sun shines warm,
And the Babe leaps up on his Mother's arm :—
   I hear, I hear, with joy I hear !   50
   —But there's a Tree, of many, one,
A single Field which I have looked upon,
Both of them speak of something that is gone :

---

32. Heart of May, the joyous influence of Spring.

IV. He tries to sympathise with the universal joy ; but his eye falls upon certain objects which had been familiar to him in youth, and which suggest the former melancholy thought.

36. Blessed, happy.

38. Jubilee, rejoicing, season of joy. Heb. *yobel*, a shout of joy. 'The heavens rejoice in sympathy with your joy.'

40. Coronal, wreath, chaplet. Lat. *corona*, a crown. At Greek and Roman banquets garlands of flowers were worn by the guests. 'My head hath its coronal' means therefore, 'I am present in spirit at your festival.' ——**Its** refers to 'festival;' the coronal is one that is appropriate to the festival, that marks him out as a guest.

42. Oh [it would be an] **evil day !** ——**Sullen**, gloomy, sad : lit. solitary. Lat. *solus*, alone.

43. Herself is the object of 'is adorning.'

45. Culling, gathering. Fr. *cueillir* —Lat. *colligere*, to collect ; *con*, with ; *legère*, to gather.

51. But = 'though I am disposed to participate in the joy of nature, yet . . .' ——**Of many, one**, one particular tree out of many.

The pansy at my feet
Doth the same tale repeat :   55
Whither is fled the visionary gleam ?
Where is it now, the glory and the dream ?

V.

Our birth is but a sleep and a forgetting :
The Soul that rises with us, our life's Star,
  Hath had elsewhere its setting,   60
  And cometh from afar :
  Not in entire forgetfulness,
  And not in utter nakedness,
But trailing clouds of glory do we come
  From God, who is our home :   65
Heaven lies about us in our infancy !
Shades of the prison-house begin to close
  Upon the growing Boy,
But He beholds the light, and whence it flows
  He sees it in his joy ;   70
The Youth, who daily farther from the east
  Must travel, still is Nature's Priest,

---

54. **Pansy,** heart's-ease, the 'thought-flower.' Fr. *penser*, to think. Lat. *pensare*, to ponder, from *pendere*, to weigh.

55. **The same tale,** that is, of 'something gone.' The pansy has no longer the brilliancy it had.

56. **Visionary gleam,** dream-like vividness and splendour (cf. line 5). This line is paraphrased in the next.

V. The poet proceeds to account for this feeling. Our soul, when it is born into this world, does not begin life for the first time ; it comes from a former life with God, and brings with it something of the glory of heaven, which, however, fades with advancing years.

58. **A sleep and a forgetting** must be taken as *one* complement of 'is.'

59. **Our life's star.** As a star must set to one hemisphere before it rises in the other, so the soul has left the heavenly world before it appears in this.

64. **Trailing.** M.E. *trailen*, to draw along ; *traile*, the train of a dress. Low Lat. *trahale*, a train. Lat. *trahere*, to draw.——**Clouds of glory,** glorious clouds. The allusion is to the radiance of sunrise, which gradually fades away.

67. **Shades of the prison-house,** the gloom of this earthly existence. By this metaphor the joyous freedom of the heavenly home is forcibly contrasted with the absorbing cares and anxieties of this earthly life. Cf. Milton's *Comus* : 'With low-thoughted care, confined and pestered in this pinfold here' (line 6).

69. **But** = still.——**Whence it flows,** its source ; a noun clause, object of 'beholds.'

71. **Who** = although he.——**The east,** the point of rising ; infancy.

72. **Priest,** minister. A.S. *preost,*

And by the vision splendid
Is on his way attended ;
At length the Man perceives it die away, 75
And fade into the light of common day.

VI.

Earth fills her lap with pleasures of her own ;
Yearnings she hath in her own natural kind,
And even with something of a Mother's mind,
And no unworthy aim, 80
The homely Nurse doth all she can
To make her Foster-child, her Inmate Man,
Forget the glories he hath known,
And that imperial palace whence he came.

VII.

Behold the Child among his new-born blisses, 85
A six years' Darling of a pigmy size !

---

from Lat. *presbyter*. Gr. *presbyteros*, elder. The youth is Nature's Priest, because he is admitted to the sanctuary of nature, is privileged to approach the divinity.

75. It, the vision splendid.

VI. Earth tries with its pleasures to make the soul forget its former state.

77. Fills her lap, produces in abundance.——Pleasures of her own, earthly pleasures, as opposed to the joys of the heaven from which we come.

78. Yearnings, longings. A.S. *gyrnan*, to desire.——In her own natural kind, of a kind natural to earth. Earth creates desires which only earthly things can satisfy.

81-84. Homely, humble. Man's true home is amid the glories of heaven ('the imperial palace'); here he is an inmate in the house of a foster-mother, Earth ('homely nurse'),

who entertains for him almost a motherly love, and would make him forget his high descent, and become attached to herself.

82. Foster-child. A.S. *fostrian*, to nourish, bring up : *fóstor*, nourishment, allied to *fóda*, food.

84. Palace. Fr. *palais*. Lat. *palatium*, the residence of Nero on the *Palatine* Hill at Rome.

VII. The Child himself helps to obliterate his early impressions by imitating the occupations of his elders.

85. New-born blisses, pleasures of earth ; these are new to him—his former joys were those of heaven.

86. Pigmy, dwarf-like, small. Gr. *Pygmaioi*, the Pigmies, fabulous dwarfs of the length of a *pygmé*, that is, 13½ inches, the distance from the elbow to the knuckles ; *pygmé*, a fist.

See, where 'mid work of his own hand he lies,
Fretted by sallies of his mother's kisses,
With light upon him from his father's eyes!
See, at his feet, some little plan or chart,   90
Some fragment from his dream of human life,
Shaped by himself with newly-learned art ;
     A wedding or a festival,
     A mourning or a funeral,
       And this hath now his heart,   95
     And unto this he frames his song :
       Then will he fit his tongue
To dialogues of business, love, or strife :
     But it will not be long
     Ere this be thrown aside,   100
     And with new joy and pride
The little Actor cons another part;
Filling from time to time his 'humorous stage'
With all the Persons, down to palsied Age,
That Life brings with her in her equipage ;   105
     As if his whole vocation
     Were endless imitation.

87. **Work of his own hand**, the toys, brick house, &c., with which he amuses himself.

88. 'Frequently interrupted in his play by his mother's caresses.'—— **Sallies**, sudden outbursts. Lat. *salire*, to leap.

89. 'While his father gazes on him with fond loving eyes.'

90. **Plan or chart**, an arrangement of his playthings intended to represent an actual scene.

91. 'Some incident in human life as he fancies it to be.'——**Fragment** is in apposition to 'plan or chart.'

93, 94. These lines stand in apposition to 'fragment.'

95. 'And this amusement now occupies his whole attention, and his song varies with the gay or solemn character of his play.'

97. **Then**, at another time. 'He

will play the merchant, the lover, or the soldier, holding imaginary conversation suited to each character.'

100. **This** = this too.

102. **Cons another part**, studies another *rôle* or character. *Con* is from A.S. *cunnan*, to know.

103–105. These lines refer to the famous passage in *As You Like It*, II. 7 : 'All the world 's a stage.'—— **His humorous stage** = his little world. The world is called a humorous stage, because in it are exhibited the humours of men, that is, their whims, follies, and caprices.

104. **Persons**, *dramătis persŏnæ*, that is, characters represented.

105. **Equipage**, train, retinue. O. Fr. *equiper*, to furnish; Icel. *skipa*, to set in order.

106. 'As if the whole purpose of his being were constant imitation of others.'

VIII.

Thou, whose exterior semblance doth belie
    Thy Soul's immensity;
Thou best Philosopher, who yet dost keep   110
Thy heritage, thou Eye among the blind,
That, deaf and silent, read'st the eternal deep,
Haunted for ever by the eternal mind—
    Mighty Prophet! Seer blest!
    On whom those truths do rest,   115
Which we are toiling all our lives to find,
In darkness lost, the darkness of the grave;
Thou, over whom thy Immortality
Broods like the Day, a Master o'er a Slave,
A Presence which is not to be put by;   120
Thou little Child, yet glorious in the might
Of heaven-born freedom on thy being's height,
Why with such earnest pains dost thou provoke
The years to bring the inevitable yoke,
Thus blindly with thy blessedness at strife?   125
Full soon thy Soul shall have her earthly freight,

VIII. The child, as retaining something of heavenly light, is the best philosopher. Why then should he, still conscious of his 'heaven-born freedom,' seek to anticipate the bonds of custom—the burdens and cares that life too surely brings?

108. 'Thou little child, whose outward appearance presents such a contrast to' . . .

110. **Who** = for thou.——**Yet** = still; implying that the heritage is afterwards lost. The child is the '*best* philosopher,' because his intuitions reveal to him truths which man with difficulty retains or recovers.

112. [Though] **deaf and silent.**——**The eternal deep**, the deep riddle of eternity.

114. The child is a prophet and seer, because he apprehends something more of truth than is visible to older men.

115. 'With whom those truths still remain.'——**Rest** may have the meaning of 'broods' in line 119.

119. **Broods**, rests, completely covers and envelops, as daylight does the objects of nature.——Supply 'like' before 'master,' and before 'presence' in the next line.

120. 'A presence that cannot be got rid of.'

121. 'Who, on thy being's height, art still glorious,' &c. Childhood, being nearest to heaven, is the mountain-top from which we descend into the darkening 'vale of life.' The child, yet radiant with the light of heavenly 'freedom,' invites the 'yoke' of earthly bondage.

123. 'Why take such pains to anticipate the burdens which life too surely brings, thus blindly opposed to thy happiness?'

125. **Blindly** modifies the adjective phrase 'at strife.'

126. **Freight**, burden. Swedish *frakt*, a cargo.

And custom lie upon thee with a weight,
Heavy as frost, and deep almost as life !

IX.

O joy ! that in our embers
Is something that doth live,   130
That nature yet remembers
What was so fugitive !
The thought of our past years in me doth breed
Perpetual benediction : not indeed
For that which is most worthy to be blest ;   135
Delight and liberty, the simple creed
Of Childhood, whether busy or at rest,
With new-fledged hope still fluttering in his breast :—
Not for these I raise
The song of thanks and praise ;   140
But for those obstinate questionings
Of sense and outward things,
Fallings from us, vanishings ;
Blank misgivings of a Creature
Moving about in worlds not realised,   145

127. **Custom,** daily round of duty.

128. Custom is not a weight that *crushes;* like frost, it renders torpid, and sends its chilling and deadening influences to almost the very roots of being.

IX. It is matter for thankfulness that even in middle life we can recall the blessed feelings of childhood, and in some measure enter into them again.

129. O [it is a] **joy that . . . .** ——Embers, ashes. A.S. *æmyrian,* embers. The fire of infancy burns out, leaving but a few sparks in the embers of our later life.

'Even when this freshness of insight has passed away, it occasionally happens that sights or sounds of unusual beauty or carrying deep associations— a rainbow, a cuckoo's cry, a sunset of extraordinary splendour—will renew for a while this sense of vision and

nearness to the spiritual world.' Myers, *Wordsworth.*

134. **Benediction,** gratitude and praise.——[I do] **not indeed** 'raise the song of thanks and praise' (line 140) **for that which,** &c.

135. **Most,** in a very high degree. ——**To be blest,** to be regarded as matter for thanksgiving.

136. **Delight** (= joy), **liberty** (= sense of freedom), **creed** (faith), are in apposition to 'these' in line 139.

141. **But** [I raise the song of thanks] **for . . .** ——Questionings of sense, doubts as to the real existence of sensible objects.

145. **Not realised,** ideal. Wordsworth tells us that in his boyhood he was often unable to think of external things as having external existence, and communed with all that he saw as something not apart from, but inherent in, his own immaterial nature. Many times, while going to school, he grasped

High instincts before which our mortal Nature
Did tremble like a guilty thing surprised :
    But for those first affections,
    Those shadowy recollections,
     Which, be they what they may,   150
Are yet the fountain-light of all our day,
Are yet a master-light of all our seeing ;
    Uphold us, cherish, and have power to make
Our noisy years seem moments in the being
Of the eternal Silence : truths that wake,   155
     To perish never ;
Which neither listlessness, nor mad endeavour,
     Nor Man nor Boy,
Nor all that is at enmity with joy,
Can utterly abolish or destroy !   160
     Hence in a season of calm weather
     Though inland far we be,
Our Souls have sight of that immortal sea
     Which brought us hither,
      Can in a moment travel thither,   165
And see the Children sport upon the shore,
And hear the mighty waters rolling evermore.

X.

Then sing, ye Birds, sing, sing a joyous song !
    And let the young Lambs bound
    As to the tabor's sound !   170
We in thought will join your throng,

at a wall or tree to assure himself that the world was not an illusion. It seemed 'falling away, vanishing,' leaving him, as it were, in a world not realised.

147. **Surprised**, taken by surprise.

148. **But** [I raise the song of thanks] **for.**——**First affections**, early instincts or emotions.

151. 'The source of all our light in after-years.'

152. **Master-light**—the light that explains all that we see. Cf. 'master-key.'

154. **Noisy**, with all their din and commotion.——**Moments**, that is, but moments, moments and nothing more.

157. **Listlessness**, indifference.——**Mad endeavour**, eager and foolish efforts.

158. **Man, Boy**, for manhood, boyhood.

161. 'And thus it is that in times of quiet thought in our later years we can still behold that ocean of eternity ' . . .

X. Therefore, again, the poet will rejoice with rejoicing nature, though the early radiance is gone beyond recall.

Ye that pipe and ye that play,
Ye that through your hearts to-day
Feel the gladness of the May !
What though the radiance which was once so bright   175
Be now for ever taken from my sight,
   Though nothing can bring back the hour
Of splendour in the grass, of glory in the flower ;
     We will grieve not, rather find
     Strength in what remains behind ;   180
     In the primal sympathy
     Which having been, must ever be ;
     In the soothing thoughts that spring
     Out of human suffering ;
     In the faith that looks through death,   185
In years that bring the philosophic mind.

XI.

And oh, ye Fountains, Meadows, Hills, and Groves,
Forebode not any severing of our loves !
Yet in my heart of hearts I feel your might ;
I only have relinquished one delight   190
To live beneath your more habitual sway.
I love the Brooks which down their channels fret,
Even more than when I tripped lightly as they ;
The innocent brightness of a new-born Day
     Is lovely yet ;   195
The clouds that gather round the setting sun

184. Comp. *Tintern Abbey*, lines 90–93. Early in 1805, Wordsworth had lost his beloved brother John, and, as he tells us, 'that deep distress had humanised his soul.' The sorrow that chastens and subdues is a source of spiritual strength and benefit.

185. The faith that looks forward to another and a better life beyond 'the darkness of the grave.'

186. The calm, serene, and cheerful mood of the matured mind.

XI. Though his childish delight in nature is gone, the poet can in some respects feel and understand the grandeur of natural objects more fully than in childhood, and with a heart matured by the human sympathies of riper years, he finds everything radiant with a moral meaning.

188. Forebode. A.S. *fore*, before ; *bodian*, announce. 'Do not imagine that our friendship is at an end.'

189. 'Still, even now, in the inmost recesses of my being, I feel the influence you exert.'

190. Only, qualifying 'one.'——One delight, the joy connected with the 'visionary gleam' of nature in childhood. 'One' is emphatic, and is contrasted with 'habitual' in the next line.

196. To him natural phenomena

Do take a sober colouring from an eye
That hath kept watch o'er man's mortality;
Another race hath been, and other palms are won.
Thanks to the human heart by which we live,   200
Thanks to its tenderness, its joys, and fears,
To me the meanest flower that blows can give
Thoughts that do often lie too deep for tears.

CHARACTER OF THE HAPPY WARRIOR.

[Towards the close of 1805, all England was mourning the loss of her greatest naval hero, 'the adored, the incomparable Nelson.' The news of Trafalgar had profoundly touched the heart of Wordsworth in his quiet home at Grasmere; and, taking the great admiral as his type of the ideal hero, he composed this short but noble poem, containing a masterly portrait, which, as has been said, may fitly 'go forth to all lands as representing the English character at its height.']

WHO is the happy Warrior? Who is he
That every man in arms should wish to be?
—It is the generous Spirit, who, when brought
Among the tasks of real life, hath wrought
Upon the plan that pleased his boyish thought: 5
Whose high endeavours are an inward light
That makes the path before him always bright:
Who, with a natural instinct to discern
What knowledge can perform, is diligent to learn;

have now a moral significance. The glories of sunset, for example, suggest to him the sobering thought that even the mightiest and most illustrious of men and of nations have here no permanent abode: one generation passes away, and leaves to another its struggles and its triumphs.

200. Thanks [be] to . . .

2. Man in arms, warrior.

3. Generous, noble, magnanimous. Lat. *generōsus*, noble-minded; lit. of noble origin; *genus*, birth. That 'the child is father of the man' was never more strikingly exemplified than in the case of Nelson. His whole career manifests that daring and impetuous spirit, that gentleness, generosity, and heroic honour, which characterised his boyhood.

6. High endeavours, lofty aims and aspirations. 'Endeavour,' from M.E. *dever*, *devoir*, duty, with Fr. prefix *en* (Lat. *in*); Lat. *debēre*, to owe. Chaucer has the phrase 'to do his dever,' that is, his duty.

8. Instinct, power of mind independent of instruction or experience. Lat. *instinctus*, an impulse; *instinguere*, to goad on, instigate.

Abides by this resolve, and stops not there,   10
But makes his moral being his prime care ;
Who, doomed to go in company with Pain,
And Fear, and Bloodshed, miserable train !
Turns his necessity to glorious gain ;
In face of these doth exercise a power   15
Which is our human nature's highest dower ;
Controls them and subdues, transmutes, bereaves
Of their bad influence, and their good receives :
By objects, which might force the soul to abate
Her feeling, rendered more compassionate ;   20
Is placable—because occasions rise
So often that demand such sacrifice ;
More skilful in self-knowledge, even more pure,
As tempted more ; more able to endure
As more exposed to suffering and distress ;   25
Thence, also, more alive to tenderness.
—'Tis he whose law is reason ; who depends
Upon that law as on the best of friends ;
Whence, in a state where men are tempted still
To evil for a guard against worse ill,   30
And what in quality or act is best
Doth seldom on a right foundation rest,

10. **Abides by,** adheres to; A.S. *abidan,* await.

11. **Prime,** first, chief; Lat. *primus,* first.

12. **Doomed,** fated, obliged ; lit. condemned ; A.S. *dóm,* judgment; *deman,* to judge.

13. **Train,** retinue, companions. Fr. *trainer,* to trail along ; Lat. *trahêre,* to draw.

14. **His necessity,** the unavoidable fate or obligation referred to in the two previous lines.

16. **Dower,** endowment, gift. Fr. *douaire,* dowry ; Lat. *dotare,* to endow; *dos, dotis,* a dowry. The 'highest dower' is the power of controlling circumstances, and drawing benefit ('glorious gain') even from things evil.

17. **Transmutes,** converts, changes into something of a different nature.

—— **Bereaves,** deprives; A.S. *bí-, reáfian,* to despoil, strip; *reófan,* to deprive.

19. **Abate her feeling,** grow callous or indifferent. The ideal hero should be gentle and humane ; his must be a heart that melts and does not harden at the sight of another's woe. The almost womanly tenderness of Nelson was shown on many occasions.

21. **Placable,** easily appeased, forgiving. Lat. *placare,* to appease.

24. **As,** in proportion as.

27. **Reason,** as opposed to passion, caprice, or self-interest.

29. **Whence** = hence, and so . . .

30. 'To do or to tolerate wrong in order to protect themselves against a greater wrong.'

31. And [where] **what.**——**Quality,** nature, character.

He labours good on good to fix, and owes
To virtue every triumph that he knows :
—Who, if he rise to station of command, 35
Rises by open means ; and there will stand
On honourable terms, or else retire,
And in himself possess his own desire ;
Who comprehends his trust, and to the same
Keeps faithful with a singleness of aim ; 40
And therefore does not stoop, nor lie in wait
For wealth, or honours, or for worldly state ;
Whom they must follow ; on whose head must fall,
Like showers of manna, if they come at all :
Whose powers shed round him in the common strife, 45
Or mild concerns of ordinary life,
A constant influence, a peculiar grace ;
But who, if he be called upon to face
Some awful moment to which Heaven has joined
Great issues, good or bad for human kind, 50
Is happy as a Lover ; and attired
With sudden brightness, like a Man inspired ;
And, through the heat of conflict, keeps the law
In calmness made, and sees what he foresaw ; ⋈

34. He is not one who does evil that good may come; all his success is achieved by worthy means.

36. Open, without concealment or deception, honest; opposed to 'secret,' 'clandestine,' 'underhand.'

37. Or else [he will] retire.—— Else = 'if he cannot retain his position honourably.'

38. His 'desire' is to maintain his integrity under all circumstances, to be *honourably* great, if great at all. He does not lose his desire; it remains with him, when he resolves to retire rather than sacrifice it.

39. 'Who understands the nature of the duties intrusted to him.'

40. With a singleness of aim, with simple sincerity of purpose, with no other end in view.

43. They, that is, 'wealth, honour, and worldly state. He does not eagerly seek them; they follow him as a necessary consequence of his noble deeds.

44. Like showers of manna, unsolicited, without effort of his own. The manna was 'rained from heaven,' Exod. xvi.

47. Peculiar, appropriate; Lat. *peculiaris*, one's own; *peculium*, private property. —— Grace, dignity.

50. Issues, results, consequences. O. Fr. *issir*, to depart; Lat. *exire*, to go out. Cf. 'event,' outcome; Lat. *ex, venire*, to come.

51, 52. No words could better describe the aspect of Nelson—his exhilaration of spirit and confidence of success—at Aboukir, Copenhagen, and Trafalgar.

54. Sees what he foresaw, the result realises his anticipations.

Or if an unexpected call succeed,   55
Come when it will, is equal to the need :
—He who, though thus endued as with a sense
And faculty for storm and turbulence,
Is yet a Soul whose master-bias leans
To home-felt pleasures and to gentle scenes ;   60
Sweet images ! which, wheresoe'er he be,
Are at his heart ; and such fidelity
It is his darling passion to approve ;
More brave for this, that he hath much to love :—
'Tis, finally, the Man, who, lifted high,   65
Conspicuous object in a Nation's eye,
Or left unthought-of in obscurity—
Who, with a toward or untoward lot,
Prosperous or adverse, to his wish or not—
Plays, in the many games of life, that one   70
Where what he most doth value must be won :
Whom neither shape of danger can dismay,
Nor thought of tender happiness betray ;
Who, not content that former worth stand fast,
Looks forward, persevering to the last   75
From well to better, daily self-surpassed :
Who, whether praise of him must walk the earth
For ever, and to noble deeds give birth,
Or he must fall, to sleep without his fame,
And leave a dead unprofitable name—   80

---

56. **Come when it will,** a complex concessive clause.

57. **Endue,** an older spelling of 'endow,' from Lat. *dotare*, to endow; *dos, dotis,* a dowry. 'Though endowed by nature with powers which find their fittest exercise in the midst of storm and turbulence.'

59. **Master-bias,** strong inclination.

60. **Home - felt,** felt at home, domestic.

61. It is said that Nelson, in the midst of storm and war, never lost his craving for the green fields and quiet pleasures of his home.

65. **Who** [whether he is] **lifted high.**

69. **To his wish** or **not** [to his wish], adj. phrase, qualifying 'lot.'

72. **Dismay,** discourage ; O. Fr. *desmayer;* Fr. *des* (Lat. *dis*) ; A.S. *mugan,* to be able.

76. **Self-surpassed,** reaching every day a higher degree of 'worth ;' qualifying 'who' in line 74. The sentiment is that of Longfellow in the *Psalm of Life* :

> 'So to act that each to-morrow
> Find us farther than to-day.'

77. 'Whether his fame is to be world-wide and immortal, inciting other men to glorious deeds.'

80. A **dead unprofitable name,** a name which does not affect for good the sentiments or acts of others.

Finds comfort in himself and in his cause;
And, while the mortal mist is gathering, draws
His breath in confidence of Heaven's applause:
This is the happy Warrior; this is He
That every Man in arms should wish to be.   85

RESOLUTION AND INDEPENDENCE.

[This poem was written when Wordsworth was thirty-seven years of age.   In
it he tells how, one bright morning after a night of wind and rain, walking
across a moor, he fell into dejection and despair as he thought of the miserable
reverses which have befallen poets, who are naturally in youth the happiest of
men; and how he was rescued from this sombre mood and recalled to sentiments of 'resolution and independence' by casually making the acquaintance
of an old and decrepit man—a leech-gatherer—who in spite of loneliness and
poverty retained his piety, cheerfulness, and fortitude.]

I.

THERE was a roaring in the wind all night;
The rain came heavily and fell in floods;
But now the sun is rising calm and bright;
The birds are singing in the distant woods;
Over his own sweet voice the Stockdove broods;   5
The Jay makes answer as the Magpie chatters:
And all the air is filled with pleasant noise of waters.

II.

All things that love the sun are out of doors;
The sky rejoices in the morning's birth:
The grass is bright with raindrops—on the moors   10

82. **Mortal mist**, the mist or shadow of death.
83. **Applause**, approval, commendation.

1. 'A calm, bright morning has followed a night of tempestuous wind and rain, and nature is again radiant with beauty and gladness.'
4. **Distant woods**, the immediate scene being a wild barren moor.
5. **Stockdove**, the wood-pigeon. Of this bird the poet has elsewhere said, 'His voice was buried among trees,' referring to the bird's love of solitude.   On this passage Wordsworth remarks: 'By the intervention of the metaphor *broods*, the affections are called in by the imagination to assist in marking the manner in which the bird reiterates and prolongs her soft note, as if herself delighting to listen to it, and participating of a still and quiet satisfaction, like that which may be supposed inseparable from the continuous process of incubation.'
8. **Out of doors**, abroad, enjoying the sunshine.
9. What may seem a commonplace personification has here a special

The hare is running races in her mirth;
And with her feet she from the plashy earth
Raises a mist; that, glittering in the sun,
Runs with her all the way, wherever she doth run.

III.

I was a Traveller then upon the moor,   15
I saw the hare that raced about with joy;
I heard the woods and distant waters roar;
Or heard them not, as happy as a boy:
The pleasant season did my heart employ:
My old remembrances went from me wholly;   20
And all the ways of men, so vain and melancholy.

IV.

But, as it sometimes chanceth, from the might
Of joy in minds that can no farther go,
As high as we have mounted in delight
In our dejection do we sink as low;   25
To me that morning did it happen so:
And fears and fancies thick upon me came;
Dim sadness—and blind thoughts, I knew not, nor could
        name.

V.

I heard the skylark warbling in the sky;
And I bethought me of the playful hare: 30
Even such a happy Child of earth am I;
Even as these blissful creatures do I fare;

significance. The poet's soul is responsive to the varying moods of nature. The emotions that stir within him are in sympathy with outward phenomena. His soul *does* 'rejoice in the morning's birth' (line 9); but soon his mood changes, and depressing thoughts turn his joy into melancholy (line 27).

18. [Being] **as happy as a boy** [is happy], **I heard them not.** A pervading sense of happiness in sympathy with nature renders him unconscious of the sounds.

19. **Season,** time, weather.——**Employ,** occupy, engross.

20, 21. The poet for the moment forgets all the painful experiences of the past, and the sad frivolities of social life.

22. **Chanceth,** happens. 'Exalted to the highest pitch of delight by the joyousness and beauty of nature, we may sometimes become depressed to the lowest dejection and despair.'

27. **Fancies,** imaginings, forebodings.——**Thick,** in great numbers.

28. **Dim,** vague.——**Blind,** dark. He is unable to tell either the source or the nature of his gloom and despondency.

30. **Me** is reflexive = myself.

32. **Fare** (A.S. *faran*, to go). The poet's experience is the same as that of the happy creatures around him.

Far from the world I walk, and from all care ;
But there may come another day to me—
Solitude, pain of heart, distress, and poverty. 35

VI.

My whole life I have lived in pleasant thought,
As if life's business were a summer mood ;
As if all needful things would come unsought
To genial faith, still rich in genial good ;
But how can He expect that others should 40
Build for him, sow for him, and at his call
Love him, who for himself will take no heed at all ?

VII.

I thought of Chatterton, the marvellous Boy,
The sleepless Soul that perished in his pride :
Of Him who walked in glory and in joy 45
Following his plough, along the mountain-side :
By our own spirits are we deified :
We Poets in our youth begin in gladness ;
But thereof come in the end despondency and madness.

VIII.

Now, whether it were by peculiar grace, 50
A leading from above, a something given,

33. 'Far from the haunts of men and the cares which intercourse with the world involves.'

34. **Another**, of an opposite character. 'Now nature wears its brightest aspect, but storms may again mar its beauty : so to me, now happy and free from anxiety, a day of gloom and distress may shortly come.' The words in line 35 are in apposition with 'day' (line 34).

37. **A summer mood**, all bright and sunny.——**Mood**, a state of mind. A. S. *mod*, disposition.

39. **Genial** (cf. *Tintern Abbey*, line 113) has two meanings : 1, cheerful ; 2, producing cheerfulness. It is used in both senses in this line. 'To cheerful faith, which always brings with it an abundance of those blessings which promote the enjoyment of life.'

42. **Who** has its antecedent in 'he' (line 40).

43. His melancholy springs from the reflection that many poets, who have begun their career in gladness, have fallen upon evil days and died in privation. ——**Thomas Chatterton**, a youthful poet of great promise (1752–1770). The frenzy of a frustrated ambition tortured his young heart, and led him to poison himself in a mean garret in London where he had lodged for some time in a state of destitution.

45. The allusion is to Burns, the ploughman poet (1759–1796). 'Sickness and debt cast heavy clouds on the closing scenes of his short pathetic life.'

47. 'Poetic genius is consciously allied to the divine.'

50. **Grace**, favour. The poet re-

Yet it befell that, in this lonely place,
When I with these untoward thoughts had striven,
Beside a pool bare to the eye of heaven
I saw a Man before me unawares: 55
The oldest man he seemed that ever wore gray hairs.

IX.

As a huge stone is sometimes seen to lie
Couched on the bald top of an eminence ;
Wonder to all who do the same espy,
By what means it could thither come, and whence ;   60
So that it seems a thing endued with sense :
Like a sea-beast crawled forth, that on a shelf
Of rock or sand reposeth, there to sun itself ;

X.

Such seemed this Man, not all alive nor dead,
Nor all asleep—in his extreme old age :   65
His body was bent double, feet and head
Coming together in life's pilgrimage ;
As if some dire constraint of pain, or rage
Of sickness felt by him in times long past,
A more than human weight upon his frame had cast.   70

gards the manner in which he is rescued from his despondency almost as an interposition of Providence.

53. **Untoward**, perverse, troublesome.

54. **Bare**, exposed, without the shelter of vegetation.

57–63. On the complex comparison in this stanza Wordsworth himself has the following remarks : ' In these images, the conferring, the abstracting, and the modifying powers of the Imagination, immediately and mediately acting, are all brought into conjunction. The stone is endowed with something of the power of life to approximate it to the sea-beast ; and the sea-beast is stripped of some of its vital qualities to assimilate it to the stone : which intermediate image is thus treated for the purpose of bringing the original image, that of the stone, to a nearer resemblance to the figure and condition of the aged Man.'

58. **Couched**, lying.——**Bald**, bare.——**Eminence**, rising-ground.

59. **Wonder**, in apposition to ' stone.'

60. This line consists of two co-ordinate noun-clauses depending on the verbal force of the noun ' wonder.'

62. **Shelf**, ledge, flat projecting layer.

64. **All**, wholly, entirely. With ' seemed' connect 'in his extreme old age.'

67. **In life's pilgrimage**, in the course of his long journey through life.

68. **Dire constraint**, dreadful and irresistible power.——**Rage**, violence.

70. ' A burden heavier than men are commonly called upon to bear.'

XI.

Himself he propped, limbs, body, and pale face,
Upon a long gray staff of shaven wood :
And, still as I drew near with gentle pace,
Upon the margin of that moorish flood
Motionless as a cloud the old Man stood,   75
That heareth not the loud winds when they call :
And moveth all together, if it move at all.

XII.

At length, himself unsettling, he the pond
Stirred with his staff, and fixedly did look
Upon the muddy water, which he conned,   80
As if he had been reading in a book :
And now a stranger's privilege I took :
And, drawing to his side, to him did say,
' This morning gives us promise of a glorious day.'

XIII.

A gentle answer did the old Man make,   85
In courteous speech which forth he slowly drew :
And him with further words I thus bespake,
' What occupation do you there pursue ?
This is a lonesome place for one like you.'
Ere he replied, a flash of mild surprise   90
Broke from the sable orbs of his yet-vivid eyes.

XIV.

His words came feebly, from a feeble chest,
But each in solemn order followed each,
With something of a lofty utterance drest—

72. **Shaven,** polished with the plane.

74. **Moorish flood,** the pool in the moor.

75. **Motionless** is subjective complement of ' stood.'

76. **Heareth,** obeys. The cloud remains stationary.

77. **All together,** in a mass, without being broken up.

78. **Himself unsettling,** changing his position, moving.

80. **Conned,** examined carefully. A.S. *cunnian*, to test ; *cunnan*, to know.

82. A stranger's privilege is the right to ask for information.

87. **Bespake,** addressed. The prefix *be* makes intransitive verbs transitive.

91. **Yet-vivid,** still bright notwithstanding his age and infirmity.

94. **Lofty utterance,** dignified mode of expression.

Choice word and measured phrase, above the reach   95
Of ordinary men ; a stately speech ;
Such as grave Livers do in Scotland use,
Religious men, who give to God and man their dues.

XV.

He told, that to these waters he had come
To gather leeches, being old and poor :   100
Employment hazardous and wearisome !
And he had many hardships to endure :
From pond to pond he roamed, from moor to moor ;
Housing, with God's good help, by choice or chance ;
And in this way he gained an honest maintenance.   105

XVI.

The old Man still stood talking by my side ;
But now his voice to me was like a stream
Scarce heard ; nor word from word could I divide :
And the whole body of the Man did seem
Like one whom I had met with in a dream ;   110
Or like a man from some far region sent,
To give me human strength, by apt admonishment.

XVII.

My former thoughts returned : the fear that kills ;
And hope that is unwilling to be fed ;

95. **Choice**, well-chosen, suitable.
——**Measured**, deliberate.

97. **Grave Livers**, men of serious life. Scottish peasants of a religious cast have long been favourably known for the solemn and appropriate language in which they converse on serious topics.

100. **Leeches** (A.S. *læce*, a physician) are worm-like animals that suck blood. Formerly they were much used in blood-letting. Medicinal leeches are found in pools and swamps, and many people used to earn a livelihood by gathering them.

101. **Employment** is in apposition with the preceding noun-clause. This stanza consists of one principal clause

'He told,' and four subordinate clauses.

104. ' Obtaining shelter for the night either in houses previously selected or wherever he might chance to find accommodation.'

106. **Talking**, telling his story. *Talk* is a frequentative form of *tell*.

107. The poet's mind is so struck by his apparently supernatural meeting with the old man that he scarcely listens to his story.

112. **Human**, of a man.——**Apt**, suited to his state of mind.

113. **Fear that kills**, ' the anticipation of evil which deprives the soul of all vigour and vitality.'

114. ' Hope that refuses to be encouraged.'

Cold, pain, and labour, and all fleshly ills ;   115
And mighty Poets in their misery dead.
—Perplexed, and longing to be comforted,
My question eagerly did I renew,
'How is it that you live, and what is it you do?'

XVIII.

He with a smile did then his words repeat ;   120
And said, that, gathering leeches, far and wide
He travelled ; stirring thus about his feet
The waters of the pools where they abide.
'Once I could meet with them on every side ;
But they have dwindled long by slow decay ;   125
Yet still I persevere, and find them where I may.'

XIX.

While he was talking thus, the lonely place,
The old Man's shape, and speech—all troubled me :
In my mind's eye I seemed to see him pace
About the weary moors continually,   130
Wandering about alone and silently.
While I these thoughts within myself pursued,
He, having made a pause, the same discourse renewed.

XX.

And soon with this he other matter blended,
Cheerfully uttered, with demeanour kind,   135
But stately in the main ; and when he ended,
I could have laughed myself to scorn to find
In that decrepit Man so firm a mind.
'God,' said I, 'be my help and stay secure ;
I 'll think of the Leech-gatherer on the lonely moor !'   140
     1807.

115. **Fleshly**, bodily.
118. **Renew**, repeat.
122. **Thus**, 'as I had seen him do.'
125. **Long**, for a long time.
127-131. The poet's mind is still so troubled by painful reflections that he hardly realises the actual presence of the old man.
133. 'After a pause, he repeated his story.'

134. 'He spoke cheerfully of other matters.' He is not occupied entirely with his own sad experiences.
136. **Stately**, with dignity.——In **the main**, on the whole.
137. 'Contrasting my own despondency with his fortitude, I could have felt ashamed.'
139. **Stay**, support.——**Secure**, sure, reliable.

[Wordsworth closes an account of his feelings in writing Resolution and Independence with these words : ' I cannot conceive a figure more impressive than
that of an old man like this, the survivor of a wife and ten children, travelling
alone among the mountains and all lonely places, carrying with him his own
fortitude, and the necessities which an unjust state of society has laid upon
him. You speak of his speech as tedious. . . . It is in the character of the
old man to tell his story, which an impatient reader must feel tedious. But,
good heavens ! such a figure, in such a place ; a pious, self-respecting, miser-
ably infirm and pleased old man, telling such a tale !']

ON THE POWER OF SOUND.

I.

THY functions are ethereal,
As if within thee dwelt a glancing mind,
Organ of vision ! And a Spirit aërial
Informs the cell of Hearing, dark and blind ;
Intricate labyrinth, more dread for thought   5
To enter than oracular cave ;
Strict passage, through which sighs are brought,
And whispers for the heart, their slave ;
And shrieks, that revel in abuse
Of shivering flesh : and warbled air,   10
Whose piercing sweetness can unloose

I. The functions of Eye and Ear
contrasted. The organ of hearing is
animated by a spirit which is in communion with sounds, individual, or
combined in harmony.

1. **Functions**, duties, operations.
——**Ethereal**, spirit-like, free.

3. **Aërial**, invisible.

4. **Informs**, animates.——**Cell of
Hearing**, the internal ear.——**Blind**,
screened from observation.

1-4. The functions of the Eye are
discharged with freedom and sprightli-
ness, the indwelling spirit glancing
forth, as it were, from the organ to
meet the objects of its contemplation.
The Ear, on the other hand, is animated by a spirit which waits and
watches to receive the sounds that
visit it.

5. **Intricate labyrinth**, the cavities
of the internal ear. ——**Dread**, awe-
inspiring.

6. **Oracular cave**, the cave of an
oracle. Such caves were resorted to
by Greeks and Romans, who supposed
that from the divine inmate they
would receive guidance in their difficulties.

7. **Strict passage**, narrow gate-
way. Through it enter sounds from
various sources and of varied significance—sighs, whispers, warbled air,
&c.

8-10. The **heart** (i.e. the emotional
nature) is stirred to activity in obedience to the 'sighs' and 'whispers'
that steal through the portal of the
ear.——**Shrieks**, shrill outcries of
terror or anguish, are satisfied with

The chains of frenzy, or entice a smile
Into the ambush of despair :
Hosannas pealing down the long-drawn aisle,
And requiems answered by the pulse that beats   15
Devoutly, in life's last retreats !

II.

The headlong streams and fountains
Serve Thee, invisible Spirit, with untired powers :
Cheering the wakeful tent on Syrian mountains,
They lull perchance ten thousand thousand flowers.   20
That roar, the prowling lion's ' Here I am,'
How fearful to the desert wide !
That bleat, how tender ! of the dam
Calling a straggler to her side.
Shout, cuckoo !—let the vernal soul   25
Go with thee to the frozen zone :
Toll from thy loftiest perch, lone bell-bird, toll !
At the still hour to Mercy dear,
Mercy from her twilight throne
Listening to nun's faint throb of holy fear,   30

assailing the *flesh* and causing it to shrink and tremble.——**Revel**, delight in.

10-13. Soft melodious strains of music, entering by the ear, calm the madman's frenzy, or brighten the dark recesses where despondency lurks.— David dispelled Saul's melancholy by the music of his harp. Cf. *Congreve*: ' Music has charms to soothe the savage breast.'

14-16. ' The choral service of praise resounds through the spacious aisles of some grand cathedral, where prayers, too, chanted amid the tombs of the illustrious dead for the repose of the departed soul, quicken the religious feelings of the devout listener.'

II. The sounds of the ' still twilight hour.'

17. **Headlong**, falling from the heights.

18. **Spirit**, of Hearing.——**With untired powers**, constantly.

19. **Wakeful.** An example of ' transferred epithet.' It is the inmates who are wakeful.

20. **Lull**, soothe, quiet. Hence **lullaby** (line 32).

21. **Here I am**, a noun-sentence (or sentence-noun) in apposition to ' roar.'

22, 23. How fearful [is] that roar! . . . How tender [is] that bleat!

24. **Straggler**, one of her young that has strayed from her side.

25. ' Carry the spirit of spring to regions where spring is unknown.'

27. The **bell-bird**, a native of South America, is remarkable for its sonorous cry, which resembles the tolling of a bell. In the twilight it perches on a lofty tree, and its tolling can be heard to a great distance. It seems to call to prayer.

28-32. The close of day, being a fitting time for prayer, is dear to Divine Mercy. Then, in her convent cell, the nun kneels before the throne of Grace with holy reverence, and whis-

To sailor's prayer breathed from a darkening sea,
Or widow's cottage-lullaby.

III.

Ye Voices, and ye Shadows
And Images of voice—to hound and horn
From rocky steep and rock-bestudded meadows   35
Flung back, and, in the sky's blue caves, reborn—
On with your pastime! till the church-tower bells
A greeting give of measured glee;
And milder echoes from their cells
Repeat the bridal symphony.   40
Then, or far earlier, let us rove
Where mists are breaking up or gone,
And from aloft look down into a cove
Besprinkled with a careless quire,
Happy milkmaids, one by one   45
Scattering a ditty each to her desire,
A liquid concert matchless by nice Art,
A stream as if from one full heart.

IV.

Blest be the song that brightens

pers her feeble orisons; in his ship at sea the sailor prays, as the shades of night gather over the waters; and in her cottage home the widow's hymn of prayer is a lullaby to soothe her babe to sleep.

III. The sounds of morning and early day.

33. **Voices, sounds.——Shadows and Images of voice**, echoes.

36. **Flung back**, reflected, re-echoed. Connect: 'images flung back to hound and horn from,' &c.

37. [Go] **on with your pastime** (= merriment).

38. **Greeting**, welcome.——**Measured glee**, referring to the merry music of the marriage bells, the tones falling at regular intervals.

39. **Their**, of the echoes.——**Milder** than that of the bells. The bells welcome the bridal party; within the church, the music accompanying the marriage ceremony awakens milder echoes.

41. **Then, or far earlier.** Until 1886 the law required that marriages in England should take place between 8 A.M. and noon.

43. **From aloft**, from a rising ground.——**Cove**, sheltered recess.

44. **Careless**, free from care.——**Quire** = choir, a band of singers.

46. **Ditty**, a song; properly, the *words* of a song. Here each milk-maid sings a song suited to her own taste or fancy, but the combination of the voices seems to the listeners above such a concert of mellow sounds as could not be equalled by the most fastidious musical composer. Cf. 'The mingling notes came softened from below' (*The Deserted Village*).

IV. The cheering and strengthening power of song.

The blind man's gloom, exalts the veteran's mirth; 50
Unscorned the peasant's whistling breath, that lightens
His duteous toil of furrowing the green earth.
For the tired slave, Song lifts the languid oar,
And bids it aptly fall, with chime
That beautifies the fairest shore, 55
And mitigates the harshest clime.
Yon pilgrims see—in lagging file
They move ; but soon the appointed way
A choral *Ave Marie* shall beguile,
And to their hope the distant shrine 60
Glisten with a livelier ray :
Nor friendless he, the prisoner of the mine,
Who from the well-spring of his own clear breast
Can draw, and sing his griefs to rest.

V.

When civic renovation 65
Dawns on a kingdom, and for needful haste
Best eloquence avails not, Inspiration
Mounts with a tune, that travels like a blast
Piping through cave and battlemented tower ;
Then starts the sluggard, pleased to meet 70
That voice of Freedom, in its power
Of promises, shrill, wild, and sweet !

50. 'Cheers the dark world of the blind, increases the happiness of the old.'

51. **Unscorned** [be] . . . = let no one despise . . .

53. 'The galley-slave, chained to the oar, rows with more spirit when his oar keeps time to song.'——**Languid**, sluggish, spiritless (*transferred epithet*).

55. 'The fairest shore becomes more beautiful, the most rigorous climate more mild, from the associations called up by the music.'

57. **Pilgrims**, wending their way to some shrine. 'At first they march slowly along; but a hymn sung in chorus quickens their steps, and makes the goal of their pilgrimage shine brighter in the distance.'

59. **Ave Marie** (= Hail, Mary !), a hymn or prayer addressed to the Virgin Mary.

62. **Nor friendless** [is] **he . . . of the mine**, compelled to toil in the mine ; like the Russian prisoners in Siberia.

63. **Clear**, innocent.

V. Power of song to excite warlike and patriotic ardour, peaceful emulation, or love with its gentler emotions of hope and desire.

65. **Civic renovation**, reformation in the state. 'When reforms have been necessary and pressing, they have been aided more by the sudden inspiration of song than by the most eloquent of orations.' Witness the effect of the *Marseillaise* on the French people in the Revolution of 1792.

Who, from a martial *pageant*, spreads
Incitements of a battle-day,
Thrilling the unweaponed crowd with plumeless heads?—
Even She whose Lydian airs inspire   76
Peaceful striving, gentle play
Of timid hope and innocent desire
Shot from the dancing Graces, as they move
Fanned by the plausive wings of Love.   80

VI.

How oft along thy mazes,
Regent of sound, have dangerous Passions trod!
O Thou, through whom the temple rings with praises,
And blackening clouds in thunder speak of God,
Betray not by the cozenage of sense   85
Thy votaries, wooingly resigned
To a voluptuous influence
That taints the purer, better mind;
But lead sick Fancy to a harp
That hath in noble tasks been tried;   90
And, if the virtuous feel a pang too sharp,
Soothe it into patience—stay
The uplifted arm of Suicide;

73. 'Who is it that from a mere warlike display—the mimicry of war—can excite feelings appropriate to combatants in a real battle in the hearts of the crowd who look on unarmed?'

75. **With plumeless heads**, qual. 'crowd:' 'with heads unprotected by helmets.'

76–80. These lines answer the preceding question.

76. [It is] **even She** (viz. the Muse of Song).——**Lydian airs**, soft and tender strains. The ancients had three modes of music—Dorian (martial), Phrygian (exciting), and Lydian (tender).

79. **Shot from**, which emanate from, are inspired by.——**Graces**, the attendants on Venus ('Love'). They were Euphrosýne (the mirthful), Aglaia (the bright), and Thalìa (the blooming).

80. **Plausive**, expressing approval.

VI. Music is often employed to excite passion; its highest aim is not to minister to sensual gratification, but to calm, subdue, and elevate human emotions.

81. **Mazes**, intricate passages in musical composition.

82. **Regent**, ruler, regulator.

85. **Cozenage**, cheating by flattery. 'Let not those who passionately love music (its "votaries") be led away by the deceitful flattery of sense to surrender themselves too fondly to a seductive influence that tends to corrupt what is purest and best in human nature.'

89. **Sick**, sickly, unhealthy. 'Lead them rather to form a taste for such music as has been found to exert a healthy influence over human minds—to inspire the virtuous with patience under trial, to arrest the hand of the

And let some mood of thine in firm array
Knit every thought the impending issue needs,   95
Ere martyr burns, or patriot bleeds!

VII.

As Conscience, to the centre
Of being, smites with irresistible pain,
So shall a solemn cadence, if it enter
The mouldy vaults of the dull idiot's brain,   100
Transmute him to a wretch from quiet hurled—
Convulsed as by a jarring din;
And then aghast, as at the world
Of reason partially let in
By concords winding with a sway   105
Terrible for sense and soul!
Or, awed he weeps, struggling to quell dismay.
Point not these mysteries to an Art
Lodged above the starry pole;
Pure modulations flowing from the heart   110
Of divine Love, where Wisdom, Beauty, Truth,
With Order dwell, in endless youth?

VIII.

Oblivion may not cover
All treasures hoarded by the miser, Time.
Orphean Insight! truth's undaunted lover,   115

suicide, to uphold the martyr and patriot in their time of need.'

94. **Mood,** mode, form of expression. ——**Knit in firm array,** strengthen and sustain.

95. **Impending,** near at hand.—— **Issue,** crisis, the consequences of their actions.

VII. Conscience, the voice of God in man, will sometimes wake the most hardened criminal to all the horrors of remorse; so music will sometimes, with dread effect, awake intelligence in the idiot's brain. Does not this prove the divine origin of music?

99. **Cadence,** strain of music.

100. **Mouldy vaults,** because long untenanted by thought.

102. **Convulsed, aghast** (line 103),

awed (line 107)—qualify **wretch** (line 101), and represent the effects of the music on the idiot.

105. **Sway,** power.

109. 'Having its abode in Heaven.'

110. **Modulations,** variations of sound.

VIII. Music is divine in its origin, and all-powerful in its effects.

115. **Insight,** power of acute observation. Insight, in spite of difficulties, searches for the treasures of truth which have been hoarded by Time. ——**Orphean,** such as Orpheus had. Orpheus, a mythical Greek hero, was the first musician and poet among the ancient Greeks, having received the lyre from Apollo himself. Men and

To the first leagues of tutored passion climb,
When Music deigned within this grosser sphere
Her subtle essence to enfold,
And voice and shell drew forth a tear
Softer than Nature's self could mould.   120
Yet *strenuous* was the infant Age:
Art, daring because souls could feel,
Stirred nowhere but an urgent equipage
Of rapt imagination sped her march
Through the realms of woe and weal: 125
Hell to the lyre bowed low: the upper arch
Rejoiced that clamorous spell and magic verse
Her wan disasters could disperse.

IX.

The GIFT to king Amphion
That walled a city with its melody   130
Was for belief no dream;—thy skill, Arion!

beasts, trees and rocks, were said to have been moved by his strains.

116. First leagues, earliest combinations.——Tutored, brought under control: opposed to 'wild, ungoverned.' ——Climb, ascend, go back to. It is 'Insight' that is addressed.

117. Grosser sphere, matter. (Contrast with 'subtle essence.')

118. Subtle, fine, spiritual.—— Essence, being, nature.——Enfold, enclose.

119. Shell, lyre. The tortoise-shell was used to form the sounding-board of the lyre.

121. Strenuous, vigorous and daring.

123. 'A glowing fancy, attending the Art of Music, carried it with daring flight into the regions both of Hell and Heaven.'

126-128. These lines refer to the effects of the music of Orpheus. His wife Eurydice having died, he followed her into the abodes of Hades, and by the charms of his lyre, prevailed on Pluto (the God of Hell) to restore her to him. Those, too, who were being tormented there for their crimes on earth ('the upper arch') were, for the time, relieved of their pains. Orpheus is also said with his 'golden tones' to have warded off all mishaps and disaster from the Argonauts, whom he accompanied on their expedition.

IX., X. Other examples of the power of music.

129. Amphion, king of Thebes, played on the lyre presented to him by Mercury with such magic skill that stones moved of their own accord and formed the city wall.

131. Arion, a famous musician of Lesbos. Returning by ship from Sicily he was attacked by the sailors, who wished to rob him. He asked to be allowed to play one strain on his lute, and when he did so dolphins, charmed by his music, came round the ship to listen. He then threw himself into the sea, and one of the dolphins carried him safely to shore. The lute and dolphin were placed among the constellations (lines 143, 144).

Could humanise the creatures of the sea,
Where men were monsters. A last grace he craves,
Leave for one chant :—the dulcet sound
Steals from the deck o'er willing waves,   135
And listening dolphins gather round.
Self-cast, as with a desperate course,
'Mid that strange audience, he bestrides
A proud One docile as a managed horse ;
And singing, while the accordant hand   140
Sweeps his harp, the master rides ;
So shall he touch at length a friendly strand,
And he, with his preserver, shine star-bright
In memory, through silent night.

X.

The pipe of Pan, to shepherds   145
Couched in the shadow of Mænalian pines,
Was passing sweet : the eyeballs of the leopards,
That in high triumph drew the Lord of vines,
How did they sparkle to the cymbal's clang !
While Fauns and Satyrs beat the ground   150
In cadence—and Silenus swang
This way and that, with wild-flowers crowned.
To life, to *life* give back thine ear :
Ye who are longing to be rid
Of fable, though to truth subservient, hear   155
The little sprinkling of cold earth that fell
Echoed from the coffin-lid ;
The convict's summons in the steeple's knell ;

132. **Humanise**, render humane.

137. **With a desperate course**, in desperation, as a last resource.

144. **In memory**, in commemoration of the event.

145. **Pan**, the shepherd-god, and inventor of the syrinx or Pandean pipes, was chiefly worshipped in Arcadia, where Mount Mænalus was his favourite haunt.

146. **Couched**, lying on the ground.

147. **Passing** = surpassingly.

148. **The Lord of vines**, Bacchus, the god of wine. He is represented as being drawn in triumph by tigers (or leopards), and accompanied by attendants who danced to the music of cymbals.——**Fauns** and **Satyrs** (rural deities) followed him, and **Silenus**, his tutor, who is represented as a jovial old man riding on an ass, and generally intoxicated.

154. The examples of the effect of sound given in IX. and X. are fables : but in real life, how impressive are certain sounds !

158. 'The tolling of the bell that summons the criminal to the scaffold.'

'The vain distress-gun,' from a leeward shore,
Repeated—heard, and heard no more !   160

XI.

For terror, joy, or pity,
Vast is the compass and the swell of notes :
From the babe's first cry to voice of regal city,
Rolling a solemn sea-like bass, that floats
Far as the woodlands—with the trill to blend   165
Of that shy songstress, whose love-tale
Might tempt an angel to descend,
While hovering o'er the moonlight vale.
Ye wandering Utterances, has earth no scheme,
No scale of moral music—to unite   170
Powers that survive but in the faintest dream
Of memory ?—Oh that ye might stoop to bear
Chains, such precious chains of sight
As laboured minstrelsies through ages wear !
Oh for a balance fit the truth to tell   175
Of the Unsubstantial, pondered well !

XII.

By one pervading spirit

159. 'The useless repetition of the signal-gun that indicates a ship in distress on a lee-shore.'——**Leeward shore**, the shore towards which the wind blows.

XI. Many and varied are the separate sounds that excite emotion. Would that these could he combined into a 'scheme or system for moral interests and intellectual contemplation !'

162. **Compass**, range.——**Swell**, increase in volume.——**Notes**, separate sounds.

166. **Shy songstress**, the nightingale.

168. **While [he is] hovering** . . .

169. **Wandering**, scattered, detached.——**Utterances**, notes, inarticulate sounds.——**Scheme**, system, plan.——**Scale**, succession of notes.

170. **To unite** is to be connected with 'scheme' or 'scale.'

171. 'The separate sounds that have influenced our moral nature and that now live only faintly in our memory.'

172. **Oh** [how I wish] **that** . . . Similarly in line 175, **Oh** [how I wish] **for** . . .

172-174. 'To be represented in a visible system or scale, such as has preserved through ages the great works of musical composers.'

175. 'Some means of accurately representing the value or importance of these powers.'

176. **The Unsubstantial**, the powers mentioned in line 171.

XII. Pythagoras taught that the motions of the universe were in accordance with certain theories of number and harmony. There is much in nature consonant with such a doctrine.

Of tones and numbers all things are controlled,
As sages taught, where faith was found to merit
Initiation in that mystery old.   180
The heavens, whose aspect makes our minds as still
As they themselves appear to be,
Innumerable voices fill
With everlasting harmony;
The towering headlands, crowned with mist,   185
Their feet among the billows, know
That Ocean is a mighty harmonist;
Thy pinions, universal Air,
Ever waving to and fro,
Are delegates of harmony, and bear   190
Strains that support the Seasons in their round;
Stern Winter loves a dirge-like sound.

XIII.

Break forth into thanksgiving,
Ye banded instruments of wind and chords;
Unite, to magnify the Ever-living,   195
Your inarticulate notes with the voice of words!
Nor hushed be service from the lowing mead,
Nor mute the forest hum of noon;
Thou too be heard, lone eagle! freed
From snowy peak and cloud, attune   200

179. **Sages**, philosophers. This was the opinion of Pythagoras of Samos, a famous Greek philosopher, 530 B.C. His doctrines were taught only to the *initiated*—i.e. a select brotherhood of disciples. He taught that the universe was a harmonious system of numbers, implying a plan and a calculating architect. It consisted of ten spheres, whose distances were so arranged that varied waves of sound were sent forth by them in their courses, and a mighty harmony evolved. This was called 'the music of the spheres.'

180. **Initiation**, admission to a select society.——**Mystery**, secret system.——**Old**, of olden times.

181. The poetic imagination loves to find in nature confirmation of the Pythagorean theory—in the Heavens, Ocean, Air, the Seasons: each has its own music.

188. **Thy pinions**, the winds.

190. **Delegates of harmony**, representatives of the universal harmony.

XIII. There *is* a scheme or scale which, in some degree, realises the wish expressed in Stanza XI.: 'All sounds may be represented under the form of thanksgiving to the Creator.'

194. **Chords**, strings.

197. **Service**—i.e. thanksgiving.—— **Lowing**, transferred epithet: it is the cattle on the mead that low.

198. **Nor mute [be] the . . .**

200. **Attune**, bring into accord with.

Milton Keynes UK
Ingram Content Group UK Ltd.
UKHW022236131223
434271UK00005B/93